Valerie Thomas and Korky Paul

Winnie's Dinosaur Day

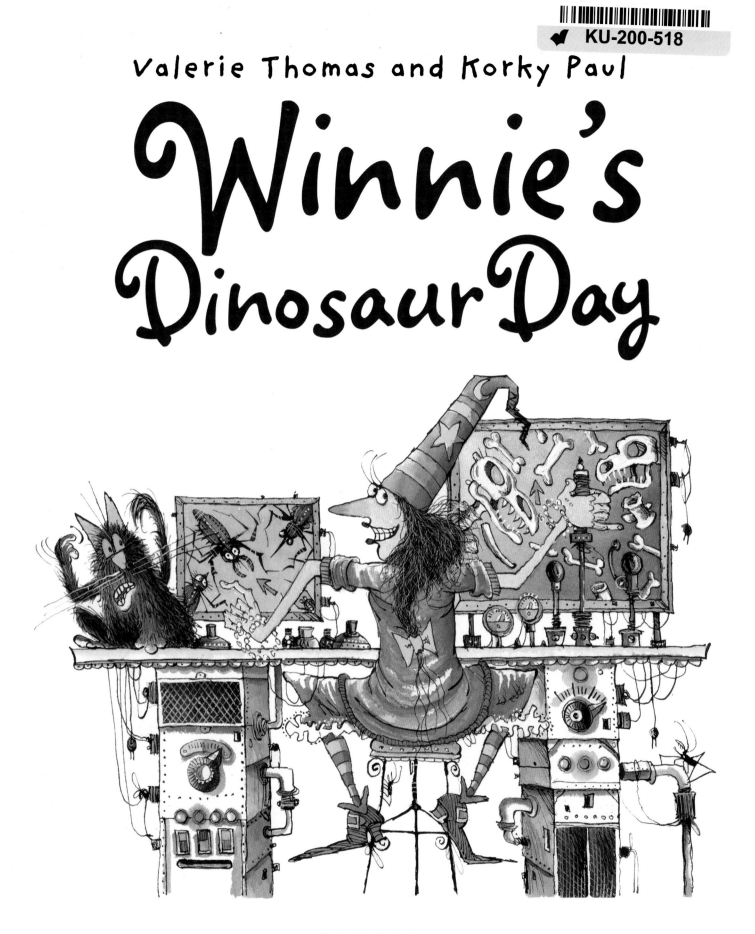

OXFORD
UNIVERSITY PRESS

Winnie the Witch and her
big black cat Wilbur loved
to visit the museum.

It was full of fascinating things.

Front endpapers by Kwon Jun-Yeong aged 4 (left) and You Eun-Jae aged 9 (right)
Back endpapers by Park Jung-Eum aged 7 (left) and Park Ji-Eun aged 7 (right)

Thank you to the children from all over Korea
who contributed pictures for the endpapers—K.P.

For beautiful Cooper—V.T.
For Teddy—K.P.

OXFORD
UNIVERSITY PRESS

Great Clarendon Street, Oxford OX2 6DP

Oxford University Press is a department of the University of Oxford.
It furthers the University's objective of excellence in research, scholarship,
and education by publishing worldwide in

Oxford New York

Auckland Cape Town Dar es Salaam Hong Kong Karachi
Kuala Lumpur Madrid Melbourne Mexico City Nairobi
New Delhi Shanghai Taipei Toronto

With offices in
Argentina Austria Brazil Chile Czech Republic France Greece
Guatemala Hungary Italy Japan Poland Portugal Singapore
South Korea Switzerland Thailand Turkey Ukraine Vietnam

Database right Oxford University Press (maker)

First published 2012

British Library Cataloguing in Publication Data available

ISBN: 978-0-19-279401-7 (hardback)
ISBN: 978-0-19-279403-1 (paperback)
ISBN: 978-0-19-279402-4 (paperback with audio CD)

2 4 6 8 10 9 7 5 3 1

Printed in Singapore

Paper used in the production of this book is a natural, recyclable product made
from wood grown in sustainable forests. The manufacturing process conforms
to the environmental regulations of the country of origin

There were bugs and beetles and
creepy crawlies and slinky snakes.

There were buttons to push,
levers to pull, and games to play.

But best of all was the dinosaur room.
Winnie and Wilbur liked to look at
the bones and footprints and models.

Ο μεγάλος παχύς ελληκός
Δεινόσαυροσμου

'I'd love to see a real dinosaur
one day,' Winnie always said.
And Wilbur always thought, 'I'm
glad I'll never see a real dinosaur.'

One day, when Winnie and Wilbur
were flying home from the library,
Winnie looked down and saw a big crowd
of people in the museum courtyard.

DINOSAUR

'Whatever's happening there?' asked Winnie,
and she flew down to have a look.

There, in the courtyard, was an enormous skeleton.
It was dinosaur week at the museum, and there
was a special competition . . .

WEEK

SPECIAL
COMPETITION.
Draw a picture
or make a model
to show what the
SKELETON
looked like when it was a
DINOSAUR.
AND WIN A PRIZE!

Winnie loved winning prizes.
She looked carefully at the skeleton.
It was very, very big, with lots of spiky bits.

Winnie couldn't decide whether to do a
picture or a model, and she couldn't decide
what the dinosaur might have looked like.

'It's too hard, Wilbur,' Winnie said.
But she really wanted to win the prize.

Then Winnie had an idea.

'Jump on my shoulder, Wilbur,' said Winnie,
and they zoomed up into the sky and back
to Winnie's house.

Winnie got out her
Big Book of Spells.
'Yes!' she said.

She shut her eyes,
stamped her foot
and shouted,

Abracadabra!

There was a flash of fire,
a great WHOOOSH . . .

and Winnie and Wilbur were back
in the time of the dinosaurs.

There were dinosaurs everywhere.
Big dinosaurs, enormous dinosaurs,
gigantic dinosaurs!

Winnie and Wilbur hid in a tree.

'Now all we have to do is find a dinosaur
that looks like the skeleton,' said Winnie.
'That should be easy.'
'Meeow,' said Wilbur.
He didn't like the time of the dinosaurs.

Winnie looked around carefully.
'There it is!' she shouted.
'Of course. It's a triceratops.
Look at its three horns, Wilbur.'
'Meeeoow!' said Wilbur.

He didn't want to look.
He wanted to go home.

Winnie got out her drawing book
and her coloured pencils.
It was much easier drawing a *real* dinosaur.

Her drawing looked *exactly* like the triceratops.
Well, it looked quite like the triceratops.

'This is an excellent drawing,' said Winnie.
'It's sure to win the prize.

But now we need to get back to the museum.
I know! The triceratops can take us.'
'Meeeoow!' said Wilbur.
He put his paws over his eyes.

Winnie picked him up, jumped onto the dinosaur's
back, waved her magic wand and shouted,

Abracadabra!

. . . and the dinosaur **WHOOSHED** off to the museum.

Professor Perkins was getting
ready to present the prize
when the dinosaur landed
in the courtyard.

Everybody was very surprised!

'Well,' said Professor Perkins,
'I think we all know who has
won the competition.'

And he gave a big shiny medal
to the triceratops.
The dinosaur was delighted.
He had never won a prize before.

Winnie didn't mind too much.

Then Winnie and Wilbur took the dinosaur home for tea.

The dinosaur didn't like sandwiches or muffins or cakes.

But he enjoyed eating Winnie's trees and her roses were delicious.

'Oh dear,' Winnie said. 'He'll eat my whole garden! It's a pity he's so big, Wilbur. He's such a nice dinosaur.'

Then Winnie had a wonderful idea. She waved her magic wand, shouted,

Abracadabra!

. . . and the **enormous** dinosaur was a _{tiny} dinosaur.

So now Winnie never has to cut her grass.
And Wilbur has a playmate that is just the right size!